# DOCTOR DUCK
# AND
# NURSE SWAN

## by Bernard Wiseman

E. P. DUTTON · NEW YORK

for Susan, Pete, Mike and Andy—

*Library of Congress Cataloging in Publication Data*

Wiseman, Bernard.
  Doctor Duck and Nurse Swan.

  Summary: Doctor Duck and Nurse Swan have a busy
day treating the various animals that come into their
office.
  [1. Animals—Fiction.   2. Medical care—Fiction.
3. Physicians—Fiction.   4. Nurses—Fiction]   I. Title
PZ7.W7802Dm   1984   [E]   83-16528
ISBN 0-525-44095-X

Published in the United States by E.P. Dutton, Inc.,
2 Park Avenue, New York, N.Y. 10016

Published simultaneously in Canada by
Fitzhenry & Whiteside Limited, Toronto

Editor: Ann Durell   Designer: Claire Counihan

Printed in Hong Kong by South China Printing Co.
10 9 8 7 6 5 4 3 2 1   W   First Edition

"Good morning," said Doctor Duck.
Nurse Swan cried, "You are late!
Look at the CLOCK, Ductor Dock!"

Doctor Duck cried, "My name is not
Ductor Dock! It is Doctor Ductor. No—
I mean Doctor Dock! No! No!"

Nurse Swan said, "Oh, we must get
to work. Mister Eagle, please come in."

"Doctor," said Mister Eagle, "I am BALD!"
Doctor Duck said, "You are SUPPOSED to be.
You are a BALD Eagle."

"Yes," cried Mister Eagle. "I am a BALD Eagle, but I want HAIR. I want a MOP of hair!"

Doctor Duck said, "I can't give you a MOP of hair, but..."

"...here is a HAIR of MOP!"

Nurse Swan said, "Mister Catfish is next."
"Doctor," cried Mister Catfish, "I am a
CATfish, but I can't MEOW!"

Doctor Duck said, "Catfish are not
SUPPOSED to meow."

Mister Catfish asked, "What should
catfish SAY?"

Doctor Duck cried, "I DON'T KNOW!"

"I DON'T KNOW! I DON'T KNOW!
I DON'T KNOW!"

Nurse Swan said, "Mister Turkey is next."
"Doctor," said Mister Turkey, "I bump
into things."

"Well," said Doctor Duck, "take off your hat.
Then you will see where you are going."

"No! No!" cried Mister Turkey. "Then
everyone would see that I am a TURKEY!
And Thanksgiving is coming soon."

Doctor Duck said, "I will have to OPERATE!"

"I CAN SEE! I CAN SEE!"

"Miss Sheep is next," said Nurse Swan.
Miss Sheep said, "Doctor, I feel too WARM."

Doctor Duck said, "Hold this in your mouth."

"Well," said Doctor Duck, "you are NOT SICK.
I will have to OPERATE!"

Miss Sheep cried, "But you said I was NOT
SICK—"

"Yes!" shouted Doctor Duck. "That is why
I MUST OPERATE!"

"Do you FEEL BETTER now?" asked Doctor Duck.

"No!" cried Miss Sheep. "Now I feel too COLD!"

"Don't worry," said Doctor Duck. "I
know what to do."

"Mister Anteater is next," said Nurse Swan.
"Look—" cried Mister Anteater. "My nose is
too LONG! Everyone LAUGHS at me."

Doctor Duck said, "I know what to do. Get undressed."

Doctor Duck said, "Go tell everyone your nose is a LEG!"

"Mister Snake is next," said Nurse Swan.

"Doctor," cried Mister Snake, "I can't catch a ball. I can't jump rope. No one will PLAY with me."

"They will!" said Doctor Duck. "Nurse,
give me a big Band-Aid—"

"Everyone will play with a HULA-HOOP!"

Nurse Swan yawned. "Oh, it is late—
Doctor Duck, look at the CLUCK!"

"You mean CLOCK," said Doctor Duck.

"Yes," said Nurse Swan. "I mean CLOCK,
Ductor Dock."

Doctor Duck cried, "My name is not DUCTOR DOCK! My name is DOCTOR DUCTOR! No— my name is—ohhh—GOOD NIGHT!"

| DATE DUE | | | |
|---|---|---|---|
| | | | |
| | | | |
| | | | |
| | | | |
| | | | |
| | | | |
| | | | |
| | | | |
| | | | |
| | | | |
| | | | |
| | | | |
| | | | |

E
W

Wiseman, Bernard.

Doctor Duck and
Nurse Swan.

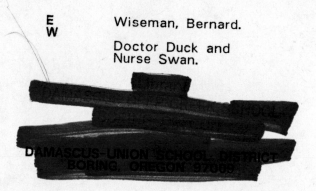